Welcome to The Giggle Club

The Giggle Club is a collection of picture books made to put a giggle into early reading. There are funny stories about a contrary mouse, a dancing fox, a turtle with a trumpet, a pig with a ball, a hungry monster, a laughing lobster, an elephant who sneezes away the jungle and lots more! Each of these characters is a member of **The Giggle Club**, but anyone can join: just pick up a **Giggle Club** book, read it and get giggling!

Turn to the checklist on the inside back cover and tick off the Giggle Club books you have read.

TEE HEE!

HA HA!

*For Amelia
and Deirdre*

First published 1996
by Walker Books Ltd
87 Vauxhall Walk
London SE11 5HJ

This edition published 1997

© 1996 Alan Baron

10 9 8 7 6 5 4 3 2

Printed in Hong Kong

This book has been typeset
in Veronan Bold.

British Library Cataloguing
in Publication Data
A catalogue record for this
book is available from the
British Library.

ISBN 0-7445-5458-6

RED FOX AND THE
Baby Bunnies

ALAN BARON

WALKER BOOKS
AND SUBSIDIARIES
LONDON • BOSTON • SYDNEY

The baby bunnies were playing hide-and-seek. "Squeak-squeak-squeak!" they giggled. They were so busy playing they didn't see Red Fox hunting for his supper.

But Red Fox saw the baby bunnies.
He ran in and out of the bushes
popping them into his sack.
"Yum, yum, yum!" he said.

Dan Dog and Tabby Cat were sitting by the lake, when they heard something squeaking.

"Red Fox has got the baby bunnies!"
 said Tabby Cat.
"To the rescue!" said Dan Dog.

After a while, Red Fox stopped for a nap.
Dan Dog and Tabby Cat crept up.
"Shh, Baby Bunnies, out you come now,"
said Dan Dog. "Red Fox is in for a big,
big surprise."

When Red Fox woke up, he heaved the
sack over his shoulder and went on.
He passed Tabby Cat in a field.
"What's in your sack, Red Fox?" she called.
"Bunnies," said Red Fox. "For supper!"

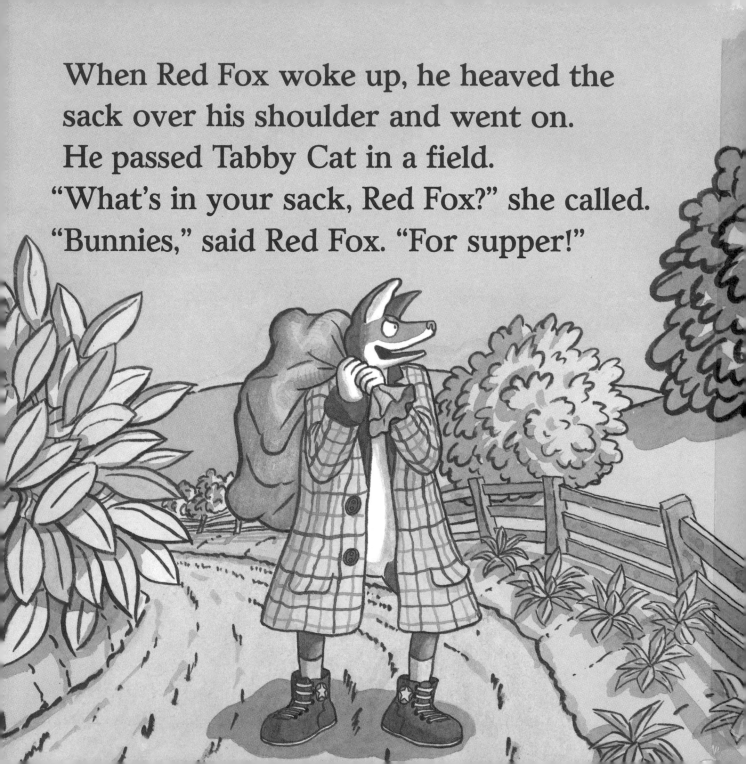

"I've got some bunnies too," said Tabby Cat.
And out popped all the baby bunnies!
"They're just like mine," said Red Fox.
"Look!" He undid the sack to show
Tabby Cat. And out jumped . . .

Red Fox stared into his sack.
"WHERE ARE *MY* BUNNIES?"
he shouted.

But Red Fox's bunnies had hopped over the hill and away. "Squeak-squeak-squeak!" they giggled.